For Emily

Neal Porter Books

Text copyright © 2022 by Philip C. Stead

Illustrations copyright © 2022 by Erin E. Stead

All Rights Reserved

HOLIDAY HOUSE is registered in the U.S. Patent and Trademark Office.

Printed and bound in June 2022 at Toppan Leefung, DongGuan, China.

The artwork for this book was created with watercolor, pencil, and colored pencil.

Book design by Erin E. Stead and Philip C. Stead

www.holidayhouse.com

First Edition

2   4   6   8   10   9   7   5   3   1

Library of Congress Cataloging-in-Publication Data

Names: Stead, Philip Christian, author. | Stead, Erin E., illustrator.

Title: The sun is late and so is the farmer / by Philip C. Stead ;
illustrated by Erin Stead.

Description: First edition. | New York : Holiday House, [2022] | "A Neal
Porter book." | Summary: "On a peculiarly long night, three farm animals
set out on a daring quest to bring the sunrise"— Provided by publisher.

Identifiers: LCCN 2022010701 | ISBN 9780823444281 (hardcover)

Subjects: CYAC: Sun—Rising and setting—Fiction. | Farms—Fiction.
Mules—Fiction. | Cows—Fiction. | Miniature horses—Fiction. | LCGFT:
Animal fiction. | Picture books.

Classification: LCC PZ7.S808566 Su 2022 | DDC [E]—dc23

LC record available at https://lccn.loc.gov/2022010701

ISBN 978-0-8234-4428-1 (hardcover)

THE SUN IS LATE
AND SO IS THE FARMER

WRITTEN BY PHILIP C. STEAD • ILLUSTRATED BY ERIN E. STEAD

NEAL PORTER BOOKS

HOLIDAY HOUSE / NewYork

A mule,
a milk cow,
a miniature horse,
standing in a barn door
waiting for the sun to rise.

There is a silence inside of everything—
inside the damp wood of the barn,
inside the farm tools hanging from the walls,
inside the dark sky overhead.
When the wind blows,
the weathervane makes a
squeak-squeak-squeak,
and there is a silence inside of that, too.

"The sun is late," says Mule.

"And so is the farmer," says Milk Cow.

"We should talk to Barn Owl," says Miniature Horse.

"Barn Owl will know what to do."

A mule, a milk cow, a miniature horse,
standing at the chicken coop where Barn Owl
likes to perch in the light of the moon.

"You are right," says Barn Owl. "The sun is late to rise."
"We will have to wake her up," says Mule.
"Or the farmer will sleep and sleep," says Milk Cow.
"And breakfast will never come," says Miniature Horse.
"Okay," says Barn Owl. "Here is what you must do . . .

Travel beyond the field full of sheep,

over the broken fence,

through the acre of tall corn,

past the sleeping giant,

all the way to the edge of the world.

THE EDGE

There you will find the sun still asleep in her bed.
Bring Rooster along—

Rooster will know what to do."

A mule, a milk cow, a miniature horse,
standing in the moonlight, so full of worry.
"We have never left the barnyard before," says Mule.
"We will have to find courage," says Milk Cow.
"We will have to be braver than we ever thought possible,"
says Miniature Horse.

A mule,
a milk cow,
a miniature horse,
walking close together.

Milk Cow touches her snout
to a sleeping sheep.
She feels the cool dew on its wool.
"What do sheep dream of?" she asks.

"They dream of other sheep," says Mule,
not knowing for sure that it is true.

A mule,
a milk cow,
a miniature horse,
afraid to be so far from home,
close their eyes and listen to the
swish-swish-swish
of the stalks against their hides.

Then there is a sleeping giant.

Miniature Horse looks back and whispers,
"What do giants dream of?"
"They dream of sheep," whispers Mule,
not knowing for sure that it is true.

Clumph-clop-clumph-clop
go the hooves in the yard of the old farmouse.
"Who's there?" calls the farmer in her bed.
The hooves make a hurry to leave.
And the farmer returns to her dream about . . .

a mule,
a milk cow,
a miniature horse,
standing at the edge of the world,
wondering about the sun.

"What does she dream of?"
asks Miniature Horse.

COCK-A-DOODLE-DOO!

"She dreams of breakfast," says Mule.

"Same as us."